The Last Priest was first performed at the King's Head Theatre, London, from 5th June to 1st July 2007, directed by Tom Cornford. The cast was:

    Julian Bird — Jean
    Maxwell Hutcheon — Claude / Voltaire / Executioner
    Angela Koo — Delphine / Pompadour

The play was conceived by Dr. Colin Brewer, and developed by Drs. Colin Brewer and Julian Bird.

The text is copyright © David Walter Hall 2007. If you would like to perform or reproduce the play, in whole or in part, please contact the author by email on davidhall@cantab.net.

ISBN 978-0-9556774-0-3

Self-published by the author.

Foreword by Dr. Colin Brewer

"Finding Father Meslier"
(programme note to the King's Head production)

I first came across Jean Meslier as a medical student in 1960. Just a brief extract in an anthology published by the British Humanist Association, of which I was a very inactive member, but I thought his story was both extraordinary and hilarious. In effect, he told his stunned parishioners in a 600-page *Mémoire* left lying by his death-bed: 'You thought I was a good priest but I never believed a word of all that religious stuff. If I'd said as much when I was alive, they'd have burned me but I'm jolly well telling you now that I'm dead. You're all deluded; there's no god, no afterlife. You're on your own. PS: monarchy sucks too but stand up to the bastards and you might just create a fairer, happier world.' Not bad for rural France in 1729. No wonder his grave is unmarked.

I mislaid the anthology and Meslier but when the Humanists reissued it in 1995, we were reunited and I started to research him. Virtually nothing has been written in English and he's little-known in France. It was a slow business but worth the effort. Born in 1664 near the future Maginot line, the only son of a small-time village weaver, he was reluctantly persuaded into the priesthood by his parents. A bright but reserved student, he became curé of the tiny village of Etrepigny in 1689 and stayed for 40 years. He kept meticulous parish records and sided with the peasants against the thuggish squire. When the archbishop of Reims ordered him to apologise, he turned the apology into a further attack and got away with it. He often waived the fees for marriages, baptisms and funerals that were his due, though a small private income may have made such generosity less remarkable. Apparently ascetic, he was twice censured for having housekeepers much younger than the usual 40-year-old minimum but claimed they were cousins and perhaps they were.

Presumably worried that his well-referenced but explosive manuscript might be destroyed, he made three copies. That any of them survived is remarkable but most of them did and expensive *samizdat* versions were soon circulating. In 1735, one came into Voltaire's hands. He deplored the 'cart-horse' style but loved the content. Still, even Voltaire had to be careful. Frenchmen could go to the galleys for selling things like that. In any case, Voltaire was a deist who thought organised religion necessary to keep the proles in order. When he published an abridged version of Meslier's manifesto in 1761, he portrayed him as a fellow deist and implied a death-bed conversion, rather than consistent disbelief. Less surprisingly, Voltaire also completely suppressed Meslier's proto-socialism, though he did credit him with being the 'most singular [of] the meteors fatal to the Christian religion'. In 1791, a statue of Meslier the anti-clerical republican was proposed but never materialised. (Just as well, perhaps. When Robespierre burnt an effigy of the Monster of Atheism, it covered the Statue of Wisdom with soot.) Meslier's *Mémoire* (aka *Testament*) remained known, if at all, only in Voltaire's travesty until a Dutch Humanist published it in 1864. Even today, it's often confused with the Baron d'Holbach's 'Common Sense', a better-written (though socialism-free) atheist polemic published anonymously in 1772 but attributed to Meslier in editions appearing after d'Holbach's perfectly-timed death in 1789.

Meslier surely deserves recognition but I thought he might also make the basis of a play, though not one that I could write myself, so theatrical friends and acquaintances were routinely encouraged to share my enthusiasm. Julian Bird liked the idea from the start and we recruited David Walter Hall to convert our ideas into a script. It's an unusual route to historical drama but we imagine Meslier wouldn't mind. It's particularly pleasing that some of the planet's tiny community of *Meslieriste* academics will be converging on the King's Head. May their numbers increase!

THE LAST PRIEST

a play about the life of Jean Meslier

by

David Walter Hall

"The Last Priest"

ACT I   SCENE 1

FANTASY #1

PROLOGUE

JEAN ADDRESSES HIS CONGREGATION FROM BEYOND THE GRAVE. IN THIS AND THE FANTASY SCENES THAT FOLLOW, THE ACTION IS ACCOMPANIED BY APPROPRIATE LIGHTING AND PERIOD MUSIC.

JEAN: Since I was forced into silence all my life, at least I shall try to talk to you now that I am dead. And so, I have written this, my Testament, to open your eyes to all the nonsense with which you were brought up and fed.

I never was inclined to frivolous beliefs or superstition, and since I never was foolish enough to adhere to any of the mysterious follies of religion, I must confess I never was inclined to practice them either, let alone to speak very highly about them, or to approve them in any way. On the contrary, I always would have willingly displayed all the contempt that I have for them, had I been allowed to speak my mind and feelings freely about them. And so, although I was easily driven into the priesthood when I was young, to please my parents who were, of course, delighted to see me there, I can I think say truly that never the sight of a worldly benefit ever inclined me to get any pleasure from the practice of a profession so full of errors and imposture.

"The Last Priest"

ACT I   SCENE 2

CLAUDE AND DELPHINE

JEAN'S PARISH HOUSE

CLAUDE SITS DRINKING CIDER FROM A BOWL WHILE DELPHINE CLEANS. SHE HAS TAKEN THE DISPLAY CROCKERY DOWN FROM A DRESSER AND PLACED THEM PRECARIOUSLY IN A STACK.

CLAUDE: And where is our hero tonight?

DELPHINE: I couldn't tell you. He's been out since this morning, same as ever. I've hardly seen that man in daylight for a month. But he usually has the sense to know when his dinner's waiting for him.

CLAUDE: Should we wait?

DELPHINE: I think so. You don't mind?

CLAUDE: I have a drink in my hand Delphine and I am happy to wait.

DELPHINE: Good. Well he shouldn't be long.

CLAUDE: Why don't you leave that for a minute? I shouldn't be the only one with a drink. Or has he given you your orders? (AS SHE DUSTS)

DELPHINE: Oh no, I doubt he knows what I do, since I wouldn't take a chance on him ever seeing the place like this. Still it must be done, and I can only do it when Father Jean is away, so if you don't mind, I'll be finished soon.

CLAUDE: He's never seen you cleaning?

DELPHINE: Not back here, no. To see him squirm with his little house all in disarray – it wouldn't be worth it. Heavens, I can picture him there in his armchair watching me now. "Oh now Delphine just be careful … don't touch the …" and all the fluttering of his gowns. Best I just let him believe – as I'm quite sure he does – that the

"The Last Priest"

ornamentation here has never been displaced since the day he in his wisdom had it set there.

CLAUDE: And what does this tell us about the good father?

DELPHINE: Well he must believe in miracles.

CLAUDE: And you work miracles?

DELPHINE: Little ones. But don't you tell Jean.

CLAUDE: And what if he should see one?

DELPHINE: A real miracle, or a me miracle?

CLAUDE: Whichever.

DELPHINE: He wouldn't believe his eyes.

CLAUDE: Well here's a notion: let us assume that the Lord in his wisdom has not presently the inclination to happily subvert the laws of nature, not at least, for our humble amusement. But, perhaps we should consider ourselves to be acting in His service...

DELPHINE: What?

CLAUDE: An act of devotion...

DELPHINE: To Jean?

CLAUDE: To our Lord. To both of them, in fact. Let's move everything around, just a bit. See if he notices.

DELPHINE: I can tell you he won't be happy.

CLAUDE: Just the cups and plates then. Put them over there.

DELPHINE: Well...

CLAUDE: We'll put those ones over here.

DELPHINE: Oh no sure he'll see it in a second.

"The Last Priest"

CLAUDE: Still. It'll be amusing?

DELPHINE SMILES

CLAUDE: Oh I knew you would.

DELPHINE: Father Claude, I'll have you know…

CLAUDE: What?

DELPHINE: (FLIRTATIOUS) I'll have nothing to do with this.

CLAUDE: Is that so?

DELPHINE: It is.

CLAUDE: Well then.

DELPHINE: Well what? (PAUSE) Get on with it. He'll be home soon.

CLAUDE: Allez.

CLAUDE PROCEEDS TO REARRANGE THE CROCKERY, SINGING CHEERFULLY. JUST IN TIME HE FINISHES AND THE DOOR IS HEARD OPENING.

"The Last Priest"

ACT I   SCENE 3

ALL THREE

JEAN ENTERS, TIRED AND MUDDY, DRESSED IN AN OLD SOUTANE.

CLAUDE:	Jean, how are you? Are they making you pull the plough now?

JEAN IS UNAMUSED.

CLAUDE:	You look tired.
JEAN:	Thank you – Claude – well, I am tired, yes, but, it's nice to see you. I thought you were coming tomorrow.
CLAUDE:	My engagements were cancelled. You don't mind…?
JEAN:	No, of course not, I'm sorry. My mind was elsewhere. Has Delphine…?
DELPHINE:	I've been making Father Claude most welcome.
JEAN:	Good.
DELPHINE:	Will you have some cider with us Father?
JEAN:	(HALF JOKING) Like a snake, you are.
CLAUDE:	Oh come on Jean. What's wrong? You can't enjoy a drink anymore? I've spent two hours on my poor old horse coming here today and my old friend – and I've had you longer than I've had the horse – won't give me a smile.
JEAN:	I've been working.
CLAUDE:	So have I. So has everyone. Now have yourself a drink.

EXHAUSTED, JEAN SMILES, ALMOST CRIES. DELPHINE POURS TWO GLASSES OF CIDER AND HANDS ONE TO JEAN.

DELPHINE:	Here you are father. So tell us then, how was it?

"The Last Priest"

JEAN: Who made this cider? Is it from the village?

CLAUDE: Good God no! I have a man in Frontignan. I brought it with me.

JEAN: From Frontignan?

CLAUDE: Oh yes. It's very good. What's wrong with the cider now?

JEAN: Nothing I'm sure. I'm just not sure how much I want to think about cider now after I have spent all afternoon with Madame Boutinot and her apples. She has begun to take an axe to her apple trees. All morning she had been hacking at them, and nearly half the orchard gone when I arrived, and only because the baker's wife had told me she seemed a little upset.

DELPHINE: <u>Was</u> she upset?

JEAN: Yes. I would say – yes. She has come to believe that the devil has taken root in her apple trees, for each fruit she says has the face of a demon. She wanted to save them – severing the trunks and praying to God to raise each fruit back into the fold. And the apples were just lying there, all of them, condemned. She had the children locked inside the house with the pigs, in case any of them should eat one. Perhaps I should laugh…

CLAUDE: Of course you should laugh.

JEAN: But these are hungry people, and Monsieur Boutinot…

CLAUDE: He can't control this woman of his…?

JEAN: He seems to have left her for their neighbour's daughter, and I hear from Madame Maille that they are on their way to Paris.

CLAUDE: (LAUGHING) I can hardly blame him. Wouldn't you do the same, Delphine?

DELPHINE: (STIFLING LAUGHTER WHILE JEAN GETS MORE UPSET) Oh, I'm sorry Jean. What did you do?

"The Last Priest"

JEAN: Well I had to take the axe from her. Then I didn't know what to do so I buried it.

DELPHINE: (LAUGHING ALOUD) You buried it?

CLAUDE: Where?

JEAN: In a ditch, by the road.

DELPHINE AND CLAUDE BOTH LAUGH AT THE IMAGE THIS SUGGESTS. JEAN SUDDENLY NOTICES THE CHANGES IN THE ORNAMENTS.

JEAN: (ANGRILY) What has happened to my cups?

DELPHINE AND CLAUDE LAUGH AGAIN AT JEAN'S EXPENSE.

CLAUDE: They're over there Jean.

JEAN: Yes, very funny isn't it?

THERE IS A STILLNESS.

CLAUDE: Look, Jean. Do you know why I'm here?

JEAN: To see your old friend. Isn't it?

CLAUDE: Well... look I'm sorry. I feel bad, I mean quite, quite bad about this really.

JEAN: Really?

CLAUDE: Look I've been asked to speak to you.

JEAN: By whom?

CLAUDE: By his grace the Arch-Bishop of Reims.

JEAN: I see. And?

CLAUDE: And he's not a very happy man.

JEAN: Well he never was, was he?

"The Last Priest"

CLAUDE: Jean, for – goodness' sake. You can't preach sermons about the Compte like that.

JEAN: What? What did I say?

CLAUDE: Delphine, no doubt you were there. What did he say?

DELPHINE: He said nothing, I'll have you know, that I wouldn't say myself, given any chance.

CLAUDE: Please, won't you make this easy for me?

DELPHINE: I don't see why. That man is an abomination.

JEAN: There you have it. The voice of the populus. I am acting within my duties to express that. Now can't we just have our dinner?

CLAUDE: Sorry Jean. You're going to have to take it back.

JEAN: Or what?

CLAUDE: Or you won't have any duties at all much longer.

JEAN: Couldn't you have tried to defend me?

CLAUDE: Sorry. What could I have done? You're lucky they asked _me_ to pass on the message, and not one of the arch-bishop's men.

JEAN: Fine.

CLAUDE: You'll retract it?

JEAN: Yes, fine. Next Sunday. Is that all?

DELPHINE: I can't believe you.

JEAN: Please Delphine.

DELPHINE: No you go ahead. And there was me thinking you actually meant it.

JEAN: Yes I did.

"The Last Priest"

DELPHINE: After what he did I should hope so. But then I'd hope you'd care enough to stand by it.

JEAN: Delphine, we can talk about this.

CLAUDE: You both must realise that it must be retracted.

JEAN: Yes.

DELPHINE: There you go again. I'll leave you men to it and go save this food.

DELPHINE EXITS.

"The Last Priest"

ACT I SCENE 4

CLAUDE AND JEAN

CLAUDE: What has happened to her?

JEAN: Her? She was practically raped by Monsieur le Compte that's all. You'll be glad at least that I lacked the decency to mention that in the sermon.

CLAUDE: (INSINUATING) So you were defending her.

JEAN: No I was defending what is right and you should know it.

CLAUDE: It's a dangerous game to be playing.

JEAN: Yes but it's a worthwhile game, and it's a game I admit I enjoy. (PAUSE) You should come more often Claude, we miss you.

CLAUDE: You know she is quite a woman. You've done well with her.

JEAN: How do you mean?

CLAUDE: I mean you've done well. You've educated her well, and she's a very passionate woman, and intelligent too, and that's the danger.

JEAN: The danger?

CLAUDE: Be careful. You know what I mean.

JEAN: Well. Delphine and I, we have a very special bond.

CLAUDE: A special bond?

JEAN: Claude, no. Now what other news have you?

CLAUDE: Where can I start? I've been offered a new position, with the Arch-Bishop of Reims.

JEAN: Oh dear. You're thinking of taking it?

"The Last Priest"

CLAUDE: Wouldn't you?

JEAN: No. Categorically.

CLAUDE: Honestly, if you were me?

JEAN: Well yes. Obviously, if I were you, and obviously you intend to take it. Do you want my blessing? I'll not try to stop you.

CLAUDE: I had hoped for your blessing actually, in a sense.

JEAN: You know what kind of man that arch-bishop is, and you know how they live there. It goes against all principle to be living with that kind of money, with people starving, and even you…

CLAUDE: No Jean. I've got to do what's best for me.

JEAN: At least you admit it.

CLAUDE: The starving people, and I see them every day, they would do the same. You know that.

JEAN: I would say to them the same thing.

CLAUDE: And they would say to you, the same thing.

JEAN: Which is?

CLAUDE: I'm taking the position in Reims.

JEAN: You're a…

CLAUDE: Oh calm down.

JEAN: No I shall not calm down.

CLAUDE: Now I've talked about this, and I think I can arrange a sinecure post for you there too, as a librarian. You'd certainly be safe from the Compte. I think it would be wise.

"The Last Priest"

JEAN: I can't believe I'm hearing this, after today, after all my effort, the rain and the idiot ditch, to hear you're off to a palace in Reims.

CLAUDE: Well done Jean. Well done for your hard work. If it makes you happy, then very good. If you want to see me in the same ditch that you're in then, then you're going to be disappointed, because I don't like mud and shit, and I've worked hard to get this.

JEAN: So you can sit back while the people starve.

CLAUDE: Starving is going to be the least of your worries if you keep on like this.

JEAN: My place is here. I shan't leave.

CLAUDE: You're a fool.

JEAN: I've heard enough of this Claude

DELPHINE ENTERS.

CLAUDE: I knew this would be a bad idea.

JEAN: Yes it most certainly was.

DELPHINE: Dinner's ready.

JEAN: Shall we eat?

CLAUDE: Yes. Let's.

THE MEN EXIT.

"The Last Priest"

ACT I   SCENE 5

FANTASY #2

VOLTAIRE

JEAN ADDRESSES HIS CONGREGATION.

JEAN: The root of all the pains that overwhelm you, and all the deceptions that keep you in the dark and under the vanity of superstition, as well as under the tyrannical laws of the rulers of this world, is nothing else, my dear friends, but that detestable policy of men. Some of them want to dominate their peers, whereas the others want to earn a reputation for their sanctity or even their divinity; they both made a clever use of not only force and violence, but also of all kinds of ruses and artifice to beguile the people, in order to achieve their goals more easily.

VOLTAIRE, WHO HAS BEEN LISTENING TO THE SERMON FROM A POINT OF DARKNESS, RISES AND INTERRUPTS.

VOLTAIRE: Not terribly well written, but I may have some use for you.

JEAN: I beg your pardon.

VOLTAIRE: I said it's not terribly well written. But I admire it all the same.

JEAN: And who are you?

VOLTAIRE: Do excuse me, monsieur, I am a writer, my name is Voltaire.

JEAN: I see. Can you help me?

VOLTAIRE: With your prose?

JEAN: I don't care about the prose.

VOLTAIRE: So how can I help you?

"The Last Priest"

JEAN: You are a writer?

VOLTAIRE: Indeed.

JEAN: And your works are published?

VOLTAIRE: I confess that I adorn all but the tawdriest of bookshelves.

JEAN: One day, perhaps then, you could bring my message to the people.

VOLTAIRE: And what *is* your message, exactly?

JEAN: You're most welcome to read it.

VOLTAIRE: I haven't the time. Please, summarise it for me.

JEAN: In that case, my arguments – are manifold...

VOLTAIRE: Yes...

JEAN: And... I suppose I begin by the belief, or indeed the assumption, as it must be an assumption, and it is the right one, of God, as it were, of the notion of a benevolent being, higher, elevated above us...

VOLTAIRE: I do hope your writing proceeds more coherently.

JEAN: You must excuse me. I have never, through all my life, uttered these words to a man before.

VOLTAIRE: Do you mutter them to trees?

JEAN: To a page, indeed, to what was once upon a time a tree. And it is somewhat different to say the words, and to hear them, being aware of how they must sound in the ears of another. You must excuse me.

VOLTAIRE: You're excused, now pray continue.

JEAN: I am an atheist. I do not believe that there is such a thing as God.

"The Last Priest"

VOLTAIRE: Very good. It is a dramatic opening.

JEAN: This is not a play.

VOLTAIRE: Riveting though it is.

JEAN: I continue to condemn all that has been constructed upon this hideous premise of man's inherent subservience, this poisonous liqueur with which all our learning is washed down, by which I mean the established church, and the laws which bind the people to it.

VOLTAIRE: I agree, but we do not need to condemn the premise to condemn such conclusions.

JEAN: I condemn it all.

VOLTAIRE: And will that make you appear more reasonable, or less?

JEAN: What should I care for appearances?

VOLTAIRE: Bene dissere est finis logices. To dispute well is the end of logic – is it not? – and you do not dispute well if you do not appear reasonable.

JEAN: But I am reasonable. There is no reason that I can see to believe in a God who answers not a single prayer, who leaves no trace of his existence on the world He is alleged to have created and whose alleged benevolent nature is contradicted a thousand times over in nature and even within the very books in which such outlandish claims are made, and seeing no reason to believe in such a thing, I, as a reasonable man, do not believe it.

VOLTAIRE: And the rest of the world is without reason?

JEAN: Yes. In this matter, yes.

VOLTAIRE: Very well, I shall take a look at it. It will do a great deal of good to have them hear such things from a man such as you. If the text is as persuasive as you are

"The Last Priest"

	passionate, I shall not hesitate to recommend to all the world that every honest man should have Father Meslier's Testament in his pocket. How does that sound?
JEAN:	It would be – impossibly – wonderful.
VOLTAIRE:	Very well then. But you'll have to get the text to Switzerland, because, well you understand the difficulties.
JEAN:	Yes.
VOLTAIRE:	Goodbye then. Good luck.

EXIT VOLTAIRE.

"The Last Priest"

ACT I   SCENE 6

JEAN AND DELPHINE

JEAN'S PARISH HOUSE

JEAN AND DELPHINE SIT READING. IT IS EVENING.

JEAN: Oh uh Christophe came by this afternoon.

DELPHINE: Did he?

JEAN: I had the impression he was looking for you.

DELPHINE: Oh.

JEAN: I told him you were at the market. I didn't put it like that, I didn't make it too obvious I mean, but I let him know where you were.

DELPHINE: I know.

JEAN: You know?

DELPHINE: Didn't he just come running down to the market to find me? And he even told me you'd sent him.

JEAN: Should I not have told him?

DELPHINE: Tell him what you want father. I can handle a man like Christophe.

JEAN: Well I'm sorry.

DELPHINE: For goodness sake, I said it was fine.

PAUSE

JEAN: He seems quite fond of you.

DELPHINE: Do we need to have this discussion?

JEAN: Is there something you want to tell me?

"The Last Priest"

DELPHINE: No father.

JEAN: I'd like to think you'd tell me...

DELPHINE: Tell you what? If I were having a secret romance with Christophe? I'd have to tell you, wouldn't I, for my own safety, because I'd clearly be on the brink of madness.

JEAN: So you're not...?

DELPHINE: Not what? Seeing Christophe? No. Am I on the brink of madness? Quite possibly.

JEAN: Very well.

THEY EACH RETURN TO THEIR READING.

I worry about you sometimes Delphine.

DELPHINE: Is it something I should know about?

JEAN: I simply mean, Delphine, that I think perhaps you might wish to marry one of these days. I wouldn't want to be keeping you locked up.

DELPHINE: Fathe... Jean please.

DELPHINE RETURNS TO SILENT READING.

JEAN: Is there something wrong?

DELPHINE: No.

JEAN: You would tell me.

DELPHINE: Of course! (PAUSE) Listen, Jean, I'm sorry. This has nothing to do with Christophe or anything. I was going to tell you anyway. Last night, when you were out, I was cleaning. I started read your book. It happened by accident.

JEAN: (GESTURING TO THE BOOK IN HIS HANDS) My book?

"The Last Priest"

DELPHINE: Not that book. The one in your study, the one you wrote. Your Testament.

JEAN: Oh dear.

THERE IS A DAUNTING SILENCE.

DELPHINE: Now is there something you'd like to tell me?

JEAN: Delphine, I'm so terribly sorry.

DELPHINE: Don't be. Were you going to show me?

JEAN: Of course I was.

DELPHINE: When?

JEAN: When the book was finished. (PAUSE) Please, I don't want this to change anything.

DELPHINE: Oh no? And were you planning on having it printed?

JEAN: Of course not.

DELPHINE: So you just wrote it – for your amusement. I can't believe that. I only read, I don't know, about a dozen pages. You sound like you want to change something.

JEAN: I really haven't given that any thought.

DELPHINE: But you were going to let me read it? Did you think about what I might do?

JEAN: I thought you would probably call me a heretic.

DELPHINE: There is no word so simple for you.

JEAN: I would not have expected you to agree with me.

DELPHINE: With the book? How could I? You'll have to forgive me, but from time to time Jean, you still do surprise me.

JEAN: Is it such a surprise?

"The Last Priest"

DELPHINE: Well I don't know. I've often felt that you are the most unlikely of priests, but perhaps that's because you are so stubborn, and because you are such a thoroughly good man. You really are. But you're a strange man. You have always loved the most transient of things more than your God.

JEAN: I take that as a compliment.

DELPHINE: Yes I knew you would. I'm sorry for reading it.

JEAN: (BLEAKLY) You shouldn't have read it, but it's okay. You can read it all when it's finished.

DELPHINE: There were dozens of pages. How long did that take you?

JEAN: I started it – a month ago. I don't know if I'll finish it.

DELPHINE: Because you're scared?

JEAN: A little, yes. But I didn't want anyone to read it.

DELPHINE: Except me.

JEAN: Well...

DELPHINE: How delightful. (PAUSE) How old was I when you took me in?

JEAN: You were seventeen.

DELPHINE: Seventeen, and I could not read nor write. And now I am twenty-eight, and I'm slowly working my way through Thomas Aquinas. Are you proud?

JEAN: Because pride's a sin? I've always cared about you.

DELPHINE: Of course you have Jean. But things have changed. You have changed, and do you know something? It's all happened in the past year, since you say you've been writing your book. You look at me differently, even if you don't know. As a woman I know.

"The Last Priest"

JEAN: What are saying?

DELPHINE: I'm practically a spinster already. And you, here you are, a man who has taught me everything I know and secretly turned and condemned all I believe is good. I just wonder where you'll lead me next? Now it seems quite clear.

IT IS NOT CLEAR TO JEAN.

DELPHINE: You know you ought to just marry me. Strange, isn't it? To have to say that to someone.

JEAN: You must be going mad.

DELPHINE: Me mad? And you with this book?

JEAN: Oh dear. Is that what you want? That's not a solution to anything.

DELPHINE: No it's a problem, but it's just a problem. It's not unovercomable.

JEAN: (ENDEAREDLY) Bless you.

DELPHINE: It's overcomable.

JEAN: Overcomable? Yes. Yes, but everything is overcomable, by reason, and by force of will and spirit, but this? This is not a thing. This is just you.

DELPHINE: It's just me?

JEAN: You're telling me that you want to marry me? I'm not made up for this. You think I should know what to do here? Take it away from me. Clean it up. Say you never said anything.

DELPHINE: Should I leave?

JEAN: No. Why? Delphine, have some sympathy for me. Don't leave. Stay. You are a silly woman, and a fool, and I hate to say it, for you are wonderful and

"The Last Priest"

	charming and intelligent, and I care for you and love you, but...
DELPHINE:	You love me?
JEAN:	But not like that.
DELPHINE:	Like what?
JEAN:	You're like a daughter.
DELPHINE:	Oh don't. Has nothing changed in your little world these ten years?
JEAN:	I'm not sure that...
DELPHINE:	Jean. It's simple. You could marry me.
JEAN:	I cannot. (PAUSE) I cannot continue with this.
DELPHINE:	Let's go to England.
JEAN:	England?
DELPHINE:	Or – Switzerland.
JEAN:	You don't understand.
DELPHINE:	Whichever. With your book. And publish it. They're protestant countries, aren't they? You can publish it there.
JEAN:	Delphine I have no desire to publish that book, not while I have my life and my sense.
DELPHINE:	Then why did you write it?
JEAN:	For truth, because it's the truth. The whole world can read it when I am dead – I hope. Truth is valuable. Truth is worthwhile. And yes it would be worth sharing, if that were only possible. And always, I thought of you. I wanted you to read it and in a way, well, I did write it for you.

"The Last Priest"

DELPHINE: Then come to England with me, and see it printed, or what will it be worth?

JEAN: Not just for you though. For Claude as well.

DELPHINE: You think he'd like it?

JEAN: No, not so much really. And you hardly like it do you?

DELPHINE: Well I haven't read all of it.

JEAN: But you are a woman of the church now. You are as dedicated to that pernicious cause as any man or woman I have seen. I wanted to educate you, as I always have, and I thought I could set you free, as I am, with my book. This talk of going to England is sheer fantasy. So you have fallen in love with me in a way, or so it seems, and that is quite understandable, I suppose. But I do not believe for a minute you are going to betray your crown and your creed for me, because you won't, because they have you, they have their grip on you like everyone else. You couldn't possibly love me, not like you think. It may seem sad to be told that, but what else can I say? I am an idiot. I have written that book for myself and for none other and it has been in vain. This past year I have wasted night after night writing the most pointless and powerless book a man ever could.

DELPHINE: So far we have established two things: that we are both idiots. I'm silly woman apparently, and a fool, and you're an idiot. I suppose being a fool is a little more amusing. And you are a man above all things and you have the conceit to tell me, a woman of some age now, that I couldn't possibly love you, or I'm not fit to marry you. And whether that is because you are an idiot, or because I'm a fool, or you have given me so much – we'll never know. Even you will admit that a fool can love an idiot...

JEAN: Delphine...

DELPHINE: And you talk like you have failed me. Because you haven't twisted me round this final pole. But you have

"The Last Priest"

	made me free, and you're right: I'm not going to turn my back on God for you. How could you even suggest it when you don't dare offer me anything in return?
JEAN:	It's not a question of trade.
DELPHINE:	I know. But you are a man and I am a woman. We are as free as God made us. We could elope to England. Get married. Publish books.
JEAN:	Do you think so?
DELPHINE:	It's all overcomable.

FOR A MOMENT THE POSSIBILITY OF THEIR ELOPING IS TANGIBLE.

JEAN:	It's not so simple.
DELPHINE:	Don't patronise me. You who cannot face himself. You who cannot see. Do you love me?
JEAN:	I am a priest. I have my duties.
DELPHINE:	You are no more a priest than the perverts who violate all the little choirboys. Your book squarely proves it. And anyway, I asked you if you loved me?
JEAN:	I cannot have this conversation.
DELPHINE:	You are a coward.
JEAN:	I am also a priest. The book will not be printed. I can see I have made a mistake, and I would ask you to stay away from my personal papers in future. Please don't mention the book to me or any of this again. Please just – leave me alone now.
DELPHINE:	That I will. I'll go to my sister's and stay there.
JEAN:	No Delphine, not like that.
DELPHINE:	I think I may have to. I'm sorry.
JEAN:	Will you come back?

"The Last Priest"

DELPHINE: I don't know.

JEAN: Do come back. You will? Won't you?

DELPHINE: I don't know. (GATHERS THINGS) Au revoir.

JEAN: (INCREDULOUS) Au revoir.

"The Last Priest"

ACT I   SCENE 7

FANTASY #3

JEAN AND MADAME DE POMPADOUR

JEAN AND POMPADOUR SIT OPPOSITE EACH OTHER AT A BANQUETING TABLE. JEAN IS UNCOMFORTABLE.

JEAN: And what do you – do?

POMPADOUR: My dear little priest, you misunderstand me. I am not burdened with – labour.

JEAN: I am aware of your privileged situation and the liberties it confers upon you. I merely wondered what, being unburdened, you are able to find to do with yourself.

POMPADOUR: I keep myself well occupied, for I am engaged in the pursuit of pleasure, and how does that make me any different from you?

JEAN: Do you read?

POMPADOUR: Why of course.

JEAN: Aristotle?

POMPADOUR: Not lately.

JEAN: Hmmm.

POMPADOUR: If you were in my position…

JEAN: I was.

POMPADOUR: With respect, good father, I doubt that.

JEAN: No, I was born, not of the privilege you enjoy, but of some, and I know what it is like. I have tasted that kind of pleasure you speak of.

POMPADOUR: I beg of you: you have not. You have never, I should imagine, ever even been to bed with a woman, so you

"The Last Priest"

      cannot speak of these matters. You cannot take
      anyone's word, nor rely upon a book. We cannot talk
      of likening pleasures. You have never been to bed
      with a woman, while I have been to bed with a king.

SHE PAUSES TO BE SURE SHE HAS BEEN HEARD.

JEAN: I am not impressed – nor am I shocked.

POMPADOUR: Well one is obliged to confess one's sins.

JEAN: It is not the sin that bothers me. "Sin" is not a word I
      understand. Most "sins" alleged to be committed in
      our world seem to be against nothing but the unholy
      laws which ensure your pleasure, madame, and so the
      very notion of sin in such a world baffles me. But I do
      confess you are immoral.

POMPADOUR: You speak like an atheist, not a priest.

JEAN: I _am_ an atheist.

POMPADOUR: I beg your pardon.

JEAN: I am an atheist.

POMPADOUR: Good heavens. For all the sins I have committed, and
      all that I intend to commit, by the grace of Jesus, I can
      at least say that I believe in God.

JEAN: Why?

POMPADOUR: Why? I may break my morals, monsieur, and do so
      most knowingly, and with every hope that my
      penitence may be light, but I believe in God, and so I
      at least have morals to break.

JEAN: In God? The God who, by way of example,
      commanded Joshua to slaughter and destroy
      "everything in the city of Canaan, both man and
      woman, young and old"; and who through Moses
      ordered His people to take vengeance on the
      Midianites, slaughtering all but the young virgins, which
      His men were to use for their pleasure; who had

"The Last Priest"

	Jephthah sacrifice his only daughter in return for the slaughter of his enemies; and who sent His own son, to Earth, to die; and no doubt you approve too of the blessed King Solomon, and his three hundred concubines? I have read such things all my life, and cannot see how this God you speak of could possibly be anything but an obstacle to any sincere morality.
POMPADOUR:	(SHOCKED) He is merciful.
JEAN:	As am I. I wish you no harm my lady, but I will not tolerate your hypocrisy, nor dismiss it as mere confusion. I am a moral man and for all you have intimated to me, I believe you may be a moral woman. But please do not insult me, yourself, or humanity itself, by insisting that for morality we must rely on anything other than the love we have in our breast for our fellow man. I must leave. Good day to you lady, and may you grow to discover a world less mysterious than the one in which you are now lost.

EXIT JEAN.

"The Last Priest"

ACT I SCENE 8

CLAUDE AND DELPHINE

CLAUDE'S PARISH HOUSE

CLAUDE IS DRAFTING A LETTER AT HIS DESK.

CLAUDE: Your grace, – May I begin by reiterating my sincerest gratitude to you for your most munificent offer? And may I continue, in the unhesitant manner of my heart's reaction, by confirming that it shall be my honour to accept the position we discussed? I hope that I may come to flourish in your service.

One does of course grow sentimental, and attached to one's parish, however small. But I assure you that I will endeavour to offer the same devotion to your invaluable work in Reims as you have witnessed me commit to the hard struggles faced here in the country.

You may recall that we discussed the issue of a housekeeper. I wonder if it would not offend your grace if I might appoint a lady of my own choosing. If you were willing to acquiesce to this slightest distortion of protocol, I'm sure your generosity would be repaid in ample measure. (THEN, TO DELPHINE, OFF) What do you think?

DELPHINE ENTERS, IN A NIGHT GOWN.

DELPHINE: About what?

CLAUDE: About the last paragraph.

DELPHINE: (DRYLY) Such admirable prose, I couldn't dare question it!

CLAUDE: (ANGRY) Were you even listening?

DELPHINE: Apparently not.

"The Last Priest"

CLAUDE: I'm asking the arch-bishop if I may appoint a domestic help of my own choosing.

DELPHINE: And?

CLAUDE: And as I've no doubt you are aware, from everything they contrived to attack Jean with over the years, a priest's domestic, if he has one at all, is supposed to be a lady of at least forty. And you're not, are you?

DELPHINE: Oh. You mean me?

CLAUDE: Yes. Will you come?

DELPHINE: To Reims?

CLAUDE: (WARMLY) Yes Delphine, I'm asking you to come with me to Reims.

DELPHINE: But what about...?

CLAUDE: Etrepigny? Father Meslier? I don't know. You might still wish to tell me what it is exactly that he's done – then perhaps I could help you answer.

DELPHINE: You don't – you don't have to know.

CLAUDE: Just another secret between the two of you?

DELPHINE: Do I have to decide – so soon?

CLAUDE: Well when else? I'm due in Reims next week, and I'd like to have this letter off today, so if you could tell me what has happened and whether you're going to be coming with me or going back there...

DELPHINE: No. I shan't go back.

CLAUDE: So you'll come with me.

DELPHINE: I can still choose – I can still choose...

CLAUDE: You're not with Jean now.

"The Last Priest"

DELPHINE: What does that mean? I am still a person. If I can breathe I can still choose.

CLAUDE: I didn't say you couldn't. You can choose to take the very generous and might I say precarious offer I'm making you, or you can choose to walk out into the streets, or of course, you can go back to Jean, but you don't want to do that do you, for mysterious reasons which we can't enter into?

DELPHINE: We can't.

CLAUDE: What on Earth has he done?

DELPHINE: You seem to care a lot. (SLYLY) You know I didn't go to bed with him.

CLAUDE HAS HAD PERSONAL EVIDENCE OF THIS.

DELPHINE MAKES FOR THE DOOR. CLAUDE GRABS HER.

CLAUDE: (INDEED, NATURALLY JEALOUS) Look, this whole ordeal upsets me too. You and Jean were like husband and wife...

DELPHINE TRIES TO LEAD CLAUDE BY THE HAND BACK TO BED.

DELPHINE: And that upsets you?

CLAUDE: Don't act like a child!

DELPHINE: I am not a child, and I am not your child any more than I am Father Meslier's.

CLAUDE: Then let's have a grown up conversation.

PAUSE

DELPHINE: Well you'll only think it's silly I suppose, or absurd, and quite perversely, well, dreadful. I can tell you, I suppose, but you can't tell another soul.

CLAUDE: I promise.

"The Last Priest"

DELPHINE: He's your oldest friend.

CLAUDE: I promise.

PAUSE

DELPHINE: Jean has written a book.

CLAUDE: What sort of book?

DELPHINE: I don't know how to describe...

CLAUDE: (JOKING) Am I in it?

DELPHINE: Ha! Claude! (LAUGHING THROUGH) Yes. In a way you are.

PEACE HAS RETURNED.

He has decided to write a book to outline his – shall we say – somewhat peculiar views on the church and the state and the monarchy of France and indeed the whole world. No one it seems has been spared, not even Jesus Himself, whom he appears to regard as having been something of a madman, roaming the desert, nibbling locusts, ranting and inventing all manner of fantasy. Has he mentioned such things to you?

CLAUDE: Not in quite so many words.

DELPHINE: Well let me continue then. He has decreed that the very foundations of our religion, of his and your sacred profession, are little more than the tools of a tyrannical plutocracy. And as for almighty God, our Holy Father who made this world, Jean has taken it upon himself to criticise His work.

You hardly seem moved. He's a liar, and a fraud. We lived, or I lived, at any rate, in harmony with the love of God, like it was a song we both heard and we moved in chorus with it. I broke my heart again and again for that man, for his work. I sacrificed so much for him, and it was all for a charade. In his mind it was a

"The Last Priest"

charade, the whole way through. I cannot understand him. Why does he still live like that?

CLAUDE: He does love his parishioners.

DELPHINE: But God is love; love comes from God.

CLAUDE: Or he did it for you? Do you think?

DELPHINE: No. Oh I don't know.

CLAUDE: You were right to leave.

DELPHINE: Thank you. Yes. (HOLDING BACK) It was hardly practical to remain in such a place.

CLAUDE: It's good sense. You don't want to be embroiled with him and everything that could to happen to him if this gets out.

DELPHINE: He didn't say he'd try to publish it.

CLAUDE: He won't have to. Things like this have a habit of making themselves known.

DELPHINE: You wouldn't report him?

CLAUDE: Of course not.

DELPHINE: Not for your career, not to please his grace, not for anything – you mustn't.

CLAUDE: I assure you. Jean is my oldest friend. I won't report him.

DELPHINE: Good.

CLAUDE: Let's just hope he doesn't try to do anything silly with it himself. Jean has never quite had the same grip on the world as you or I, because he's never quite had to. He has lived his life on silver skates fashioned from the spoon he found in his mouth. He can afford the humble life. He has it in him, and I respect him for that. And sure enough, he can afford to have his grand

"The Last Priest"

ideals. He can put them under a glass globe in his square of turf up there, and sit on his haunches as his sanity unravels before him. But let him keep it contained there, for all of our sakes. I'll be going to visit him soon enough.

DELPHINE: Don't mention any of this.

CLAUDE: I won't.

DELPHINE: No you will. You've just about said as much. You can't let him know I'm with you. I intend no offence Claude, but as sure as any man can hate, he'll hate us both for it, and for good. I feel awful enough. I've been dishonest enough...

CLAUDE: I won't tell him anything. Do you think I've no more sense than that? Now let's get back to Reims.

DELPHINE: Where?

CLAUDE: Back, as it were, to the subject of Reims. Come, be my "housekeeper".

DELPHINE: I'm not going to be any man's mistress.

CLAUDE: (HALF-JOKING) Then will you be my wife?

DELPHINE: (SARCASTIC) Would that it were possible Claude!

CLAUDE: It will be possible. These are only words. The protestants allow their ministers to marry and they seem happy enough.

DELPHINE: They're more than words, and you're not such a fool. Marriage is a sacred bond in any language.

CLAUDE: But we can make our own bonds, as sacred as we please. And I'd like you to come with me. And I'd like it if you would like to come. I'll make it work, I'll pull strings, and as for Jean, I'll lie to the man if I must, I'll tell him I saw you passing through and that you're doing well, or I'll tell him nothing at all if that's what you'd prefer. It is my desire to go to Reims, and it is my

"The Last Priest"

	humblest and most sincere desire, to have you come with me.
DELPHINE:	Yes, yes. The romantic! You are indeed made of noble stuff – but you give me so little choice.

"The Last Priest"

ACT I   SCENE 9

FANTASY #4

VOLTAIRE AND MADAME DE POMPADOUR.

JEAN SITS AT A DESK WORKING ON HIS MANUSCRIPT. ACROSS THE STAGE, IN JEAN'S MIND, ARE VOLTAIRE AND POMPADOUR.

VOLTAIRE: Madame de Pompadour. (PAUSE) Are you looking at our priest here?

POMPADOUR: Yes. Vile man.

VOLTAIRE: Do you think so?

POMPADOUR: Yes. You don't?

VOLTAIRE: I think him a fool. But he isn't vile.

POMPADOUR: What would you call him then?

VOLTAIRE: He is in fact a man of great principle. The book he is writing – is incredible.

POMPADOUR: He's an atheist…

VOLTAIRE: Very much so.

POMPADOUR: And he is writing about atheism?

VOLTAIRE: Again, yes.

POMPADOUR: I don't understand.

VOLTAIRE: How so?

POMPADOUR: You called him a fool, but you say his book is incredible.

VOLTAIRE: Most people are fools. You are a fool, most of the time. I'll bear witness to that.

"The Last Priest"

POMPADOUR: Yes, and I know you have your reasons for exempting yourself from such a judgement, mister Voltaire. But why do you condone him, the atheist? You yourself for all your attenuations of our creed have admitted as much as that belief in God is most necessary.

VOLTAIRE: And so you see why I call him a fool.

POMPADOUR: I fear you admire him a little as well.

VOLTAIRE: A man such as this has nothing to gain from believing anything but what is written. To rewrite the universe from scratch, and to do so knowing that he will never see his words published within his lifetime; you wouldn't call that admirable?

POMPADOUR: Monsieur Voltaire, decency forbids me.

VOLTAIRE: Decency has never interested me, and, frankly, I'm surprised to hear it spoken of so highly by you.

POMPADOUR: I did not speak highly of it. I am bound by it.

VOLTAIRE: Madame, excuse me if I do not deign to flatter you, but I suspect you are not. He speaks of what God means to him; I speak of what God means to me; that makes him worthy of my respect. (PAUSE) He despises the king.

POMPADOUR: And do you?

VOLTAIRE: Certainly not, but it is an interesting point of view. No I love the king as much as you do, if eh, a little less passionately.

POMPADOUR: Your respect goes a long way, as you know. It might have been interesting I suppose. It might have been interesting to have heard him speak for a little longer. I wish you'd recommended him in advance.

VOLTAIRE: If you're lucky, I may publish his book one day.

POMPADOUR: Really?

"The Last Priest"

VOLTAIRE: Maybe. But not all of it. Just the highlights. After all, he's only a fool.

"The Last Priest"

ACT I   SCENE 10

CLAUDE AND JEAN

JEAN'S PARISH HOUSE

JEAN: Claude, Claude, Claude, Claude, Claude. Welcome.

CLAUDE: Thank you.

JEAN: How are you?

CLAUDE: Well.

JEAN: Good. Good.

CLAUDE: It's so cold in here, why don't you light a fire?

JEAN: Oh, I ran out of wood. One of the farmers came and borrowed some. He said he'd come by today and pay me back with whatever he had. He must have forgotten.

CLAUDE: You know you can be too generous (IN GENERAL).

JEAN: Yes, well, oh if Delphine were still here, she'd probably march right down to the farm and carry the load back in her arms. I don't have the strength. But I never did. Anyway, what's this, more cider?

CLAUDE: Cognac.

JEAN: You're going up in the world.

CLAUDE: It's my gift, to you.

JEAN: Oh bless you Claude. If you only knew what this place was like. Look at these eyes of mine – I'm losing my sight, slowly. The town is desolated. We had a fever swept through last month and took one in five of us. More work for me I suppose. I feel like I'm a gardener now, but dragging my rake through a garden where the weeds don't even grow and... How did you hear about Delphine?

"The Last Priest"

CLAUDE: I didn't.

JEAN: She's gone, you know?

CLAUDE: Yes I did know. I said I didn't... but I didn't know until today. The innkeeper told me.

JEAN: We had a bit of an argument.

CLAUDE: I see.

JEAN: I wonder about it all, about the world, about these silly people, who sincerely believe what they see before them is the best of all possible worlds, and all is for the best.

It ought not to take a great intellect to see this world was not designed with much love in mind. Or much wisdom. Or much power. But the Bible tells them otherwise, and there they are every Sunday, captivated by every word of it, and what can I say to them? For all the good I have done, I remain a slave to the ignorance of these people. And I am as culpable as anyone else for their misery.

They don't complain, well they don't complain to me. I wonder what they pray about, whether they're all at home complaining, as they rightfully should be, as I would be. And why aren't they knocking on my door, with a disgruntled message to take to their creator? Are they simply afraid? Afraid of the divine and the noble. The divine, put there by the noble, and the nobles put there, of course, by the almighty Himself, as they so willingly believe. The farce of it – like some creature that eats its young.

CLAUDE: You're much too good at what you do. If you told them God wanted them to eat more artichokes and walk on stilts, you know they'd follow it to the letter.

JEAN: Maybe that is what I should do. We can turn this whole town into a circus act. I say "we" – I'll take responsibility of course. I'll tell them to cover their faces in mud, and dance around like savages. Maybe then

	they'll get the joke, and see the absurdity of all this, of everything.
CLAUDE:	I don't think so. The truth is they will follow, no matter what, as they always have. The Greeks had their priests and they followed their gods. The Romans were the same. The Turks have their god and we have ours.
JEAN:	So have you now lost sight of the one true faith?
CLAUDE:	Not at all. The one true faith is the one we have, it's the one that pays your salary and mine.
JEAN:	You have an interesting way of agreeing with me sometimes. The people, the people are just blinded by it. Even Delphine… She would respond to all of this with the most elegantly chosen quotation, from the Bible, or from Aquinas or Leibniz – always delighting in the humility and weakness of the human mind, beneath the infinite mysteries of the mind of the Creator. And there would be no turning her. Her gaze fixed on the light and the truth, blinded by it. For years I let myself enjoy it in her, as if it were a virtue.
CLAUDE:	I think it is.
JEAN:	Virtue is only what gives us pleasure. And we are fools when we feel too much pleasure.
CLAUDE:	Do you really believe that?
JEAN:	No. (PAUSE) I miss her.
CLAUDE:	Oh Jean I'm sorry.
JEAN:	No, please, it's not your fault she's gone. Are we going to drink this or aren't we?
CLAUDE:	Of course.
JEAN:	Well onwards then, we'll drink it at the inn in the village. The food's not good, but it's good for here. We may be poor, but we are at least still French.

"The Last Priest"

JEAN APPEARS UNSTEADY.

CLAUDE: Jean, is something wrong?

JEAN: No not at all.

CLAUDE: You don't have to drink it, but – it won't do you any harm. You'll not go to hell over a bottle of this.

JEAN: Well... (TAKES THE BOTTLE AND SMILES, AS IF THE DEVIL WERE SMILING BACK AT HIM)

CLAUDE: Now, come on. Come and let me cheer you up.

"The Last Priest"

ACT I   SCENE 11

                    FANTASY #5

JEAN ENTERS, MANUSCRIPT IN HAND AND ADDRESSES HIS
CONGREGATION.

JEAN: For those who govern or take part in the domination of
               the others, and for priests, who rule over consciences,
               or who benefit from fat revenues, you the people are
               like goldmines, or a Golden Fleece. You are like horns
               of plenty, who provide them with all kinds of goods at
               their will. This is what gives all these gentlemen the
               means to entertain themselves and have all kinds of
               amusement, while you the poor, abused by the faults
               and superstitions of religion, groan sadly, poorly and
               without protest under the yoke of the oppression of the
               great. You patiently suffer your pains, you vainly pray
               to gods and saints that will not hear you, you lose your
               time in vain devotions, you devoutly accomplish the
               penitence and mortification that you were enjoined to
               do after the vain and superstitious confession of your
               sins.

               And now you see: you poor people work like dogs day
               and night to earn your wretched living, and to cater
               lavishly for the pleasures and bliss of the very ones who
               make your lives so miserable.

                    SUGGESTED INTERVAL

"The Last Priest"

ACT II   SCENE 1

FANTASY #6

JEAN ENTERS, MANUSCRIPT IN HAND AND ADDRESSES HIS CONGREGATION.

JEAN: My dear friends, if you knew of the vanity and the foolishness of the nonsense that you are being entertained with under the pretext of religion, and if you knew how unfairly and how shamefully the tyrants that dominate you take advantage of the authority that they have inflicted upon you, you would certainly feel nothing but contempt for everything that you are told to respect and worship, and you would feel nothing but hatred and indignation towards all those who deceive you, who govern you so rudely, and who mistreat you so shamefully.

For all my weakness and my lack of spirit, I will show you the truth. I will make you see the vanity and fallacy of all the mysteries allegedly great, sane, divine and so adorable, which your priests, your preachers and your doctors compel you to believe.

As for the priests, preachers, doctors and all those who are responsible for such lies, such nonsense and such impostures, let them be scandalised and shocked as much as they like now that I am dead; let them call me an impious person, an apostate, a blasphemer and an atheist if they like; let them shower me with insults and curse me as much as they like. I do not feel embarrassed about it, it does not worry me a bit.

And as for my body, let them do whatever they want with it; let them chop it into pieces, roast it or fricassee it, even eat it, if they want, with whatever sauce they like. It will cause me no grief at all. I am out of their reach now. I no longer fear anything.

"The Last Priest"

ACT II   SCENE 2

CLAUDE AND DELPHINE

CLAUDE'S LODGINGS IN REIMS: DELPHINE'S CHAMBER

DELPHINE IS IN BED, ILL AND SLEEPING. CLAUDE ENTERS, WITH A BOWL AND A LETTER. DELPHINE AWAKENS.

CLAUDE: I've brought you some soup.

DELPHINE: Thank you. Put it there, I'll have it in a moment.

CLAUDE: And I have a letter.

DELPHINE: Yes?

CLAUDE: From Jean.

DELPHINE: Oh.

CLAUDE: Can you listen?

DELPHINE: Yes. What does he say?

CLAUDE: He says – let me read it to you:

(READING) All men – he says – however pious or saintly, become in their lives the guardians of secrets. These little lonely prisons we guard: secret thoughts, secret actions, secret lives which we live only in our hearts. And all men die, sooner or later, and it seems to me so shameful that their secrets die with them.

(READING) The church may have contrived for us the confession, and to many a man the artifice of the weekly confession sets their secrets free, and they believe, absurdly, that they are closer to the ones they have betrayed, and to God, because of it. But to us priests, the confession can only truly be seen as an ugly charade. It is not to God, and it is not to the priests that man must confess his sins. It is to his fellow man whom he has sinned against.

"The Last Priest"

(READING) It is these thoughts which have played on my mind over the past days, and they have moved me to throw caution to the wind, uncharacteristically you'll no doubt say. I've always wanted to see Reims again, so I have decided I shall pay you a long overdue visit. I do not wish to cause you any panic; my only wish is to bring us closer in friendship, and any harm that may fall my way from the hands of the arch-bishop, it will be my own fault entirely.

DELPHINE: Is he talking about me?

CLAUDE: The "secrets" – clearly.

DELPHINE: When's he coming?

CLAUDE: Well it's Tuesday today. Sunday was the first. So in the next few days. Tomorrow maybe. He doesn't seem to say for sure.

DELPHINE: Good.

CLAUDE: Good?

DELPHINE: It will be good to see him.

CLAUDE: Don't you think you should try to hide?

DELPHINE: How am I going to hide, when I can hardly get out of bed? And he's right, we shouldn't keep secrets.

CLAUDE: But we have kept secrets. He kept that book of his secret – didn't he? – and with good reason, and you and I have kept this quiet, together, and with good reason.

DELPHINE: And you propose I hide?

CLAUDE: Don't you think so?

DELPHINE: No Claude. As much as I love a farce, I can't conceive of it happening.

CLAUDE: Then what will we say?

"The Last Priest"

DELPHINE: The game is up. The game is up, so we shall tell the truth.

CLAUDE: Are you mad?

DELPHINE: I for one look forward to seeing this man again.

CLAUDE: And breaking his heart?

DELPHINE DOES NOT WANT TO BREAK JEAN'S HEART.

CLAUDE: You seem to imagine that I am the only one who is at fault here, the only one who is going to wound him, the only one who is going to incur his wrath.

DELPHINE: If only you'd let me write to him before...

CLAUDE: Let's not start.

DELPHINE: But isn't that right? He would have understood. Six months ago he would have understood, and he'd have blessed us, but now, with me like this and time so far gone, it's mockery. I knew this day would come, and we'd have to incur "his wrath".

CLAUDE: I am not afraid.

DELPHINE: Aren't you ashamed?

CLAUDE: We only did what was best.

DELPHINE: Best for us.

CLAUDE: For us and him.

DELPHINE: Well I am ashamed. And Jean is right. Secrets are no good. All that we have had, and it's been _good_, has come at a price. We are living in sin, and soon judgement will be upon us. He moves in mysterious ways.

CLAUDE: How on Earth did he find out?

"The Last Priest"

DELPHINE: Anyone could have told him. You haven't exactly been a model of discretion. I know what you talk about over dinner with the others.

CLAUDE: I do not.

DELPHINE: Not that it bothers me.

CLAUDE: I have been most discreet. You don't think it could have been your sister, or someone else you've written to?

DELPHINE: Why would she?

CLAUDE: By accident, somehow. He might have gone to look for you at her home.

DELPHINE: She wouldn't have said anything. (PAUSE) Stop looking at me like that.

CLAUDE: I'm sorry...?

DELPIHNE: Take your pity elsewhere. Silly man. Your heart was never big enough for two, and your pity now will not flow over onto me, so please, and I mean this sincerely, find yourself some solitude, and go and pray for your own soul, and leave me to pray for mine.

CLAUDE: As you wish.

EXIT CLAUDE.

"The Last Priest"

ACT II   SCENE 6

FANTASY #7

THE EXECUTIONER

AN EXECUTIONER STANDS BY A GUILLOTINE.

JEAN: An executioner?

MAN: Yes monsieur.

JEAN: Do you kill the poor? The starving and oppressed?

MAN: No. I am here to execute the mighty, who have abused their power – "until the last king is strangled with the guts of the last priest" – and I shall execute the king.

JEAN: Why?

MAN: These are your words monsieur. Don't tell me they were only rhetoric. If I had real guts to use I would use them, but we have a guillotine.

JEAN: Do you believe in God?

MAN: No.

JEAN: And in heaven?

MAN: No. I have seen enough to convince me against it.

JEAN: So how does it feel to send a man to his death?

MAN: Would you like to try?

JEAN: No. I admit I would not.

MAN: I don't blame you.

JEAN: I value life too much.

MAN: Why do you value life?

"The Last Priest"

JEAN: Interesting question.

MAN: You don't believe in God or heaven either, do you?

JEAN: No I do not.

MAN: Which means, that you believe in death. But still you value life?

JEAN: I value life in spite of death. I try to find substance in little things: in the faces of my friends, in the good that I can do. And I try to read of the great advances we make are making in the natural sciences, which fill me with wonder. I believe they offer hope for man. Is that too sentimental?

MAN: It is not sentimental, but what will these things matter when you come to die? Friendship too is mortal. What will it matter when your friends have betrayed you? The value of these things lies in the value of life, or in the longevity of friendship. And when that life is taken away, so will they become worthless to you. You are certain that you will die?

JEAN: Some day. Yes.

MAN: Then you can be certain these things will forever cease to be of value.

JEAN: Yes, but...

MAN: Now answer this: what is more valuable than life?

JEAN: Nothing, surely.

MAN: Is nothing therefore worth dying for? I disagree with you here. In the alchemy of our hearts, in the spirit world we build, some things transcend mortality: dignity, truth; some say art, some say France.

JEAN: I would say I would like to agree.

"The Last Priest"

MAN: You must agree monsieur. Nothing is ever worth living for that is not worth dying for. For everything else will be annihilated. One might simply speak of love.

JEAN: Love is worth dying for?

MAN: Precisely. And therefore, worth killing for.

JEAN: That is vanity. That is delusion.

MAN: All is vanity and delusion monsieur. Man's hope lies in his capacity to fool himself.

There is ample truth to be discovered in the world; but all of it is shallow and ephemeral. For in the world, we see there are no miracles, there is no magic. But the soul of a man is the truth in his heart, and though it is only vanity and delusion, insanity even, it is the only truth that matters when faced with Death.

To kill for love is indeed great, and French. To kill for France is greater still. Death means nothing to a life lived beyond its dominion. We must be prepared to live that life. Death is the measure of all truth. And so we must be prepared – to kill, and to die.

JEAN: And you shall die a coward.

MAN: So be it.

"The Last Priest"

ACT II   SCENE 4

JEAN AND CLAUDE

A COURTYARD IN FRONT OF CLAUDE'S LODGINGS IN REIMS

JEAN ENTERS, WITH A WALKING STICK. HE IS POORLY AND WEARS SPECTACLES. HE CALLS FOR CLAUDE WHO EVENTUALLY APPEARS IN RICH VESTMENTS PROTECTED BY AN APRON. HE HAS BEEN PAINTING.

CLAUDE: Jean. Aha! It's Jean. It's good to see you.

JEAN: Thank you. A little earlier than expected I fear.

CLAUDE: It's fine it's fine. You're lucky in fact. We thought you'd be here tomorrow maybe.

JEAN: Well I needed the boy to help me, and he had to…

CLAUDE: Of course. It's no trouble. None at all. (PAUSE) Oh look at you – how's your eyesight now?

JEAN: It's worse, but please…

CLAUDE: Jean I'm glad you could come.

JEAN: I'm glad you could have me.

CLAUDE: And your journey?

JEAN: The journey was fine, really.

CLAUDE: And how's life back home?

JEAN: It's fine, it's the usual, it's nothing like this. I still miss Delphine.

CLAUDE: Yes. Yes I know.

JEAN: I miss her, but I've given up on her now.

CLAUDE: What do you mean you've given up?

"The Last Priest"

JEAN: Well I suppose I thought she might come back, but – she could be anywhere.

CLAUDE: So you don't know?

JEAN: Know what?

CLAUDE: She's here. She's been here since… Isn't that why you're…?

JEAN: Since when?

CLAUDE: Since, since the day she left you in Etrepigny. She walked.

JEAN: She walked?

CLAUDE: You didn't know?

JEAN: No. Who would have told me?

CLAUDE: Jean. She isn't well. Has no one told you?

JEAN: No.

CLAUDE: I thought that's why you wanted to come. Sorry I assumed.

JEAN: No. Why didn't you say something when you wrote to me, or every time you came to see me?

CLAUDE: What could I have said?

JEAN: You've kept this secret for a year. What have you been doing with her?

PAUSE

CLAUDE: Come inside Jean. Come inside.

THEY MOVE INTO CLAUDE'S PARLOUR.

You know you can't stay here tonight? I wish you could but I'm having lunch with his grace tomorrow. If

"The Last Priest"

	he sees you here, there'll be questions. You're not so popular these days.
JEAN:	Really?
CLAUDE:	It's serious. There has been talk about your arrest this time, for treason. Look, about Delphine, it's, I'm so sorry you didn't know.
JEAN:	But you should have realised…
CLAUDE:	I know, I suppose I did but… Jean, listen though – Delphine is dying.
JEAN:	Is she here?
CLAUDE:	Yes she's through there but…

CLAUDE IS POWERLESS TO STOP JEAN, WHO MOVES UPSTAGE TO WHERE DELPHINE IS LYING IN BED.

"The Last Priest"

ACT II   SCENE 5

JEAN AND DELPHINE

DELPHINE'S CHAMBER

DELPHINE IS LYING WITH HER EYES CLOSED. CLAUDE REMAINS OUT OF THE SCENE.

JEAN: Oh Lord, Delphine.

DELPHINE AWAKENS.

DELPHINE: Jean? Oh Jean...

JEAN: I didn't know you were here. I had a message for Claude.

DELPHINE: He said you were coming. And it's today...?

JEAN: I wrote to him. He was expecting me.

DELPHINE: Oh well, what did he say? I take it you know what happened.

JEAN: No. Why does everyone here keep saying that?

DELPHINE: So he didn't tell you?

JEAN: I just arrived. Tell me.

DELPHINE: I was pregnant Jean.

JEAN: Oh no.

DELPHINE: Claude took me to a woman in a village, to get rid of the... it. She was a gypsy. I thought she'd be good at it. It hurt so much and I knew – I knew I wouldn't make it.

JEAN: You knew the risks?

DELPHINE: Of course. (MOCKING HERSELF) But she was a gypsy.

"The Last Priest"

JEAN: And the baby was Claude's of course...?

DELPHINE: Yes it was Claude's, but it's all my own silly fault really.

JEAN: If you'd only written to me...

DELPHINE: Of course I wanted to – but Claude wouldn't let me. He's really kept everything – under control, so I just let him get on with it.

JEAN: Really? I can't imagine you ever saying that.

DELPHINE: I know. But I'm sick. I wouldn't have thought I'd say it, but, I suppose I've changed.

JEAN: I'm sorry.

DELPHINE: Oh he's sorry too, don't get me wrong. He tells me every night. (COUGHS) I never thought I'd see you. Did you finish your Testament?

JEAN: Yes. Yes it's all sitting wrapped up in paper in my study.

DELPHINE: You'll have to publish it some day, for me. Let them hang you for it. It won't matter.

JEAN: You've still got your sense of humour.

DELPHINE: Yeah? I'm getting tired, I'm sorry. Are you going to stay the night? Can we talk more in the morning?

JEAN: I really just came to give Claude a message. I can't stay long. Claude says they may try to arrest me, and besides, I have plans.

DELPHINE: Then you must go Jean. I'll understand. You've really never changed. Every day since I left I thought about you just the same, just like you are now, with your plans and your obligations, and I read your letters to Claude, where you just talked about the village and all the people. It all made me so sad, because everything for me has been changing out of control, but you never changed. Something's different about you now

"The Last Priest"

	though. Remember – whatever happened to Madame Boutinot and her apple trees?
JEAN:	Her? Her husband came back. He's planted pears this time. They're going to be fine.
DELPHINE:	That's good. That's nice.
JEAN:	This is... Have you been happy here, with him?
DELPHINE:	Yes. Mostly.
JEAN:	Claude's not a bad man at all. He's not much of a priest...

THEY LAUGH.

DELPHINE:	He's a good man. Your plans, are they important?
JEAN:	Yes – absolutely – I'm sorry.
DELPHINE:	I love you Jean.
JEAN:	Delphine don't say that, don't end it like that.
DELPHINE:	I shall die as I choose!
JEAN:	Oh dear I'm sorry.
DELPHINE:	No, it's fine Jean. You'll never change. It's good to know, and I mean it I love you.
JEAN:	Do you understand why it's hard for me to say that?
DELPHINE:	You don't have to. I know how your life is hard.
JEAN:	Not by my choice it's not.
DELPHINE:	You're a good man. That's why it's hard. Do you forgive me?
JEAN:	Delphine you never did a thing wrong.
DELPHINE:	Now Father Meslier, that is a lie if I ever heard one.

"The Last Priest"

JEAN: I didn't blame you. You know, I always understood.

DELPHINE: And Claude, do you forgive him?

JEAN: Well I don't know, we'll see. (SINCERELY) Of course I do.

DELPHINE: I think he's your only weakness.

JEAN: You might be right.

DELPHINE: (COUGHS, WEAKLY) Jean I think you should go. I need to rest some more.

JEAN: Perhaps I could come back. We could talk more.

DELPHINE: I don't think so Jean. My time isn't long now.

JEAN: Very well.

JEAN STANDS.

DELPHINE: Oh no. Please, just... Au revoir Jean. Till we meet again.

JEAN: Au revoir.

DELPHINE: (TEASING) I'll send you my kisses from heaven.

JEAN: Delphine...

DELPHINE: Sssssshhh...

DELPHINE CLOSES HER EYES. JEAN, DEVASTATED, SLOWLY EXITS.

"The Last Priest"

ACT II   SCENE 6

JEAN AND CLAUDE

CLAUDE'S PARLOUR

JEAN MOVES DOWNSTAGE BACK INTO CLAUDE'S PARLOUR, WHEREUPON HE EMBRACES CLAUDE WITH SILENT EMOTION.

JEAN: (UPSET) Why didn't you tell me?

CLAUDE: I, I...

JEAN: (ANGRY) Why didn't you tell me? Why in God's name didn't you tell me? You were going to let her die like that and not tell me.

CLAUDE: Jean, I wanted to.

JEAN: Oh, yes...?

CLAUDE: Of course I wanted to but...

JEAN: But what?

CLAUDE: You'd have – it would have upset you and...

JEAN: You took her from me and you did this to her and she is half dead now and you were worried I would get upset.

CLAUDE: Jean be quiet. She'll hear.

JEAN: I don't care. Let her. Let her hear what her master has done. Or are you worried that the other priests will hear? Is that it? What would they say, Claude, if they knew? What? Or does everyone here have a slave they keep locked up just like her, like the king does – does the arch-bishop, does the pope? He must have dozens. Was it hard Claude? Is the first one the hardest one to lose? Or was she not even the first? Well...?

CLAUDE: Well what?

"The Last Priest"

JEAN: Tell me.

CLAUDE: Jean, you know as well as I do that I care for Delphine every bit as much as you do.

JEAN: How dare you...?

CLAUDE: I have been through a living hell because of this. Believe me.

JEAN: And long may you rot there. You are an outrage, and you are supposed to be a priest, a man of morals. But you're a hypocrite too.

CLAUDE: As are you.

JEAN: Pathetic!

CLAUDE: We're all hypocrites.

JEAN: I see. And it's all the same to you. Has she told you everything?

CLAUDE: She mentioned the book, if that's what you mean – and isn't that the reason she came here to me in the first place?

JEAN: Oh so you have lost the power of reason too now! How can you say that?

CLAUDE: Why did she come here Jean? Tell me. You can't answer can you? At least I provided what you could not.

JEAN: Wretch!

CLAUDE: And no, I did not wish for this to happen – ever, ever, ever.

THEY ARE BOTH EXASPERATED.

JEAN: You know, I was just telling Delphine how I was going to forgive you for this. How can I trust you Claude?

"The Last Priest"

CLAUDE: Please why don't you listen to me? This is not what I wanted.

JEAN: Fine. Good. What does it matter anyway?

CLAUDE: Don't dismiss this. I need you to forgive me...

JEAN: Why?

CLAUDE: ...I need to be absolved of this. Please, will you absolve me of this? You're the only one I can ask.

JEAN: I couldn't, I'm sorry.

CLAUDE: I can't go to any other priest. I'm afraid. I'm afraid who they might tell. I respect you more than any other priest Jean. I trust you more. Please.

JEAN: You don't understand. I can't absolve you of you of your sins because it wouldn't be honest. I can, I can forgive you, or try, and if it's not enough...

CLAUDE: It's not enough! You do it every day. Why can't you do it for me?

JEAN: Because it wouldn't be honest.

CLAUDE: But you do it every day.

JEAN: You know I didn't even come here for Delphine. I have to – she mentioned my manuscript...

CLAUDE: The one that's going to put us all out of a job?

JEAN: Yes.

CLAUDE: Jean, it's none of my business.

JEAN: And is she your business – her – Delphine – is she your business? And how can there be such suffering there in that room and a God alongside it? Did you ever see such a void – such an absence of any goodness? God is nowhere in that room with her; God is nowhere at all. I am an atheist.

"The Last Priest"

CLAUDE: (GOBSMACKED) Rubbish! You're a priest.

JEAN: I want you to publish the manuscript for me.

CLAUDE: And it's on atheism now? Jean I know your feelings on the church, and I don't necessarily disagree with you, but – how could I even try to print that? They'd burn me like Vanini, along with the book!

JEAN: Will you?

CLAUDE: How? When?

JEAN: When I'm dead.

CLAUDE: When you're dead? And when that's going to be?

JEAN: Claude I'm getting old, I can barely see anymore. I'm a sick man and it hurts me just to move. You can't imagine what it was like coming here for you by horse. I've finished my Testament and there's nothing left for me to do in the world. I've got a little laudanum. I sent my dog to sleep with it. The poor thing, he was as bad as me. I've enough left for three dogs, which is one of me. I'm taking it tonight, when I get home.

CLAUDE: I don't believe this. You're serious.

JEAN: Yes.

CLAUDE: And you came all this way just to tell me?

JEAN: I came to say goodbye. And seeing Delphine...

CLAUDE: I'm glad you got to see her. You know she's amazed me.

JEAN: Me too. She always did.

CLAUDE: And are you going to absolve me? I don't want to beg.

JEAN: Absolve you? Why? You don't understand, I don't believe in any of this.

"The Last Priest"

CLAUDE: It doesn't matter. You are a priest. Please.

JEAN: Yes. And apparently, you are my only weakness.

CLAUDE: What does that mean?

JEAN: It's what Delphine said.

PAUSE

CLAUDE: Will you?

JEAN AGREES.

CLAUDE: Confiteor Deo omnipotenti, et vobis fratres, quia peccavi nimis cogitatione, verbo opere et omissione: mea culpa, mea culpa, mea maxima culpa. Ideo precor beatam Mariam semper Virginem, omnes angelos et Sanctos, et vobis fratres, orare pro me ad Dominum Deum nostrum. Amen.

Forgive me Father for I have sinned. I have committed the sin of adultery. I have made a woman pregnant, and selfishly, I have coerced her into the ministrations of a *faiseuse d'anges*. I forced her to. Father Meslier, what penance must I perform?

JEAN: Return to Etrepigny. Collect the manuscript that you find in my study. Carry out the instructions I leave for you.

CLAUDE: Father Meslier...

JEAN: That shall be your penance. Do you understand?

CLAUDE: Yes Father.

JEAN: Then go in peace. In nomine patris et filiis et spiritu sanctis, amen.

CLAUDE: (RISES) If I could only talk you out of this...

"The Last Priest"

JEAN: You haven't a chance, I'm afraid. You're too late. But, you must promise me, to get the manuscript published. You owe it to me.

CLAUDE: Jean I still respect the sacraments.

JEAN: Really? Not that I want this to be...

CLAUDE: And I still respect you, more than ever. Jean, this is morbid.

JEAN: Well, yes, that's a little inevitable don't you think?

CLAUDE: And you're just going to leave?

JEAN: I must. There was always a lot of love I had for you Claude. I want you to know that. I always have. Now you've moved into this palace, and you're doing very well, and you're going to be very important some day, I'm very sure of it. I never would have, you know, because you know how I feel, but that's... It's less important now. I can see you're happy with this. I hope you're happy. That's good, good for you. You're just human, very human. In fact you are utterly, wonderfully human. No, I shall go to my death with a smile on my face, I will, and remember you and Delphine and this wonderful ridiculous tragedy.

CLAUDE: And if I may say so, you are a little bit human too sometimes, and I thank you for it. I really wish you could stay.

JEAN: I know. (PAUSE) Goodbye, old friend.

THEY EMBRACE.

CLAUDE: That's it?

JEAN: Yes. That's it. That's all there is.

CLAUDE: Please Jean.

JEAN: Adieu. Good luck.

"The Last Priest"

CLAUDE: Good bye.

JEAN EXITS.

"The Last Priest"

ACT II   SCENE 7

EPILOGUE

CLAUDE MOVES INTO A SPOT CENTRESTAGE, HOLDING A BOOK. HE ADRESSES THE AUDIENCE.

CLAUDE: And of course, he was a man of his word. I found his body lying in his bed the next morning, and the little flask under his pillow, a perfect vision of serenity. Some of the plates were broken on the shelves downstairs. I think he must have tried to clean the house before he – but in the dark and with his eyesight... Oh well. I just hope it didn't upset him too much to know he left a mess behind for me to clean up. Delphine died two days later. I never told her about Jean. I don't think it would have surprised her much to know, but it might have upset her, on the inside. I shall not try to speak of the sadness of it all. I was a man of my word too, hard as it was getting that thing to the Swiss border. I've remained a priest. And I've tried to be a good one, for Jean. It is a question of priorities, and I think Jean, in his way, would agree. I'd like to read you some of his words, the final page of his testament:

CLAUDE BEGINS READING.

It is said in one of our so-called holy and divine books that God will cast the haughty and glorious princes from their thrones, that in their place he will seat gentle and peaceful men. It is said there that he will dry out the roots of glorious nations and that he will install humble ones in their place. Who are these haughty and glorious princes of whom the so-called holy and divine books speak? People of France, they are your sovereigns, your dukes, your princes, your kings, your monarchs, your potentates. Show me, in your days, the accomplishments of these so-called divine words and cast all these proud and haughty tyrants from their thrones! Men, women, there is no God, you are alone down here. Love, help and respect each other.

CURTAIN

www.ingramcontent.com/pod-product-compliance
Ingram Content Group UK Ltd.
Pitfield, Milton Keynes, MK11 3LW, UK
UKHW041434180426
11947UKWH00007B/439